THE REAL GHOSTBUSTERS™

GHOSTS-R-US

When Slimer unwittingly releases a
particularly unpleasant family of ghosts,
the Ghostbusters team find themselves
with competition on their hands of a
ghastly ghostly kind.

Ghostbusters are here to save the world!

The second title in the Real
Ghostbuster Series.

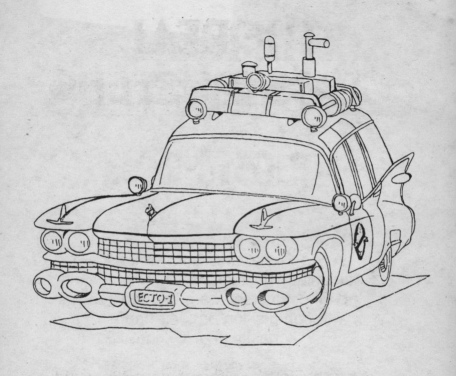

Ecto-1

THE REAL GHOSTBUSTERS™

GHOSTS-R-US

novelisation by
Kenneth Harper

Illustrated by Jon Miller

KNIGHT BOOKS
Hodder and Stoughton

First published in Great Britain by Knight Books 1988

The characters and situations in this book are entirely imaginary and bear no relation to any real person or actual happening

British Library C.I.P.

Harper, Kenneth, *1940–*
Ghosts-r-us.
Rn: Keith Miles   I. Title   II. Miller, Jon, *1947–*
823'.914[J]

ISBN 0-340-42129-0

Printed and bound in Great Britain for Hodder and Stoughton Paperbacks, a division of Hodder and Stoughton Limited, Mill Road, Dunton Green, Sevenoaks, Kent TN13 2YA (Editorial Office: 47 Bedford Square, London WC1B 3DP) by Cox and Wyman Limited, Reading, Berks. Photoset by Rowland Phototypesetting Limited, Bury St Edmunds, Suffolk.

1

Sweet Dreams

New York City never sleeps. It is alive and busy for twenty-four hours a day. Those who look after its welfare have to be on duty around the clock. They never rest.

Something could happen at any moment.

The Ghostbusters knew this only too well. They were called out regularly at the most unearthly hours. Every time they went to bed, there was a chance that they might be dragged out of it by an emergency. Ghosts haunt best at night.

They did not complain. Well, not all *that* much, anyway. They got used to it. Being hauled out in the small hours was a sort of occupational hazard. It went with the territory.

'Awwwwwwwwww!'

Egon Spengler yawned. It was almost midnight and he was up in the laboratory on the top floor at Ghostbuster Headquarters. The building had once been a fire station and a lot of its original features remained. Egon had added things which the firemen would never have recognised or understood. His laboratory was a jungle of complex equipment.

'Awwwwwwwwwww!'

A second yawn made him stand up from what he was doing. Egon Spengler was devoted to science. A tall, thin, intelligent man with a shock of white hair, he committed himself totally to the dangerous science of ghostbusting. His only hobby was collecting spores, moulds and fungus. And it was this collection that he was now tending. He started to put it away.

'Time for bed, little ones,' he said.

His third yawn was the loudest and tiredest yet.

'Eeeeeeeeaaaaaawwwww!!!!'

While Egon carefully wrapped up his precious collection, Ray Stantz was turning in for the night. Or so he hoped. The alarm bell did have a nasty habit of disturbing his slumbers.

The dormitory was also on the top floor. It was a large room with four beds in it and an amiable clutter of books, paintings, sound equipment, hanging plants, games, wardrobes, tables and chairs. A goldfish bowl stood beside one bed and its occupant swam slowly in circles looking for a watery way out. An unfinished game of chess lay on the table.

Ray Stantz sat up in bed to read an encyclopedia by the light of his anglepoise lamp. He flicked through the pages.

'Now where was I?' he asked.

The others told him that he didn't need to look at an encyclopedia because he *was* one. Ray knew just about everything there was to know about Weird Things and their equally weird history. If you asked him who haunted what in Chattanooga in 1935, or what happened to the Pasadena Phantom of 1877, or why the Galveston Ghoul of 1921 had six eyes but no nose, then he would be able to tell you.

It wasn't just his knowledge that made him such a valuable member of the team. Ray was fearless. He'd blunder happily into the unknown in the name of scientific experiment and not give a second thought to his own safety. Also, he was the mechanic among the Ghostbusters, the man with the magic hands who built all the ingenious devices that Egon dreamed up.

Ray noted something in his encyclopedia.

'Well, I never knew that!' he said.

But he did. He's just fooling you.

Turning over the page, he read on with interest.

Dr Peter Venkman was also reading. He was on the floor below in the big room that served as kitchen, lounge and dining area. It was here that the Ghostbusters relaxed if and when they got the opportunity. Like all the other rooms, it was an odd mix of the old and the new. There was plenty of modern furniture and equipment but the air of a fire station still lingered.

Peter was not reading a book or a magazine.

'Your turn,' he reminded.

'I know.'

'Hurry up then.'

'Don't rush me.'

Seated at a table, Peter was playing cards with Winston Zeddmore and trying to read his face. But Winston gave nothing away. When he played poker, he had a poker face. Peter could not guess what he held in his hand.

Peter was a bright, quick-talking character who helped to found the Ghostbusters. Though he preferred to avoid danger if possible, he never held back when the chips were down. Wise, witty and cynical, he was always good fun to have around.

But he did not like losing at cards.

'Come on, Winston.'

'I'm thinking, man.'

'You been thinking for five minutes.'

'So? I like to take my time.'

'Well, your time's up, Buddy. Play.'

Winston Zeddmore was a cheerful, happy-go-lucky man with a ready smile. Unlike the others, he had no scientific background but he made up for this with his other qualities. He was brave, loyal and very practical. When his colleagues got themselves bogged down with a problem, Winston usually took a direct approach and found a solution.

He became a Ghostbuster when he rolled up to look for a job. Any job. He didn't really mind. He got a job all right.

Busting ghosts is full-time work.

'Like me to come back in the morning?' mocked Peter.

'No, no. I'm ready now.'

'Hooray!'

'I'll raise you.'

'You'll *what*?'

'Raise you.'

They played for matchsticks rather than money. It was cheaper that way. Winston tossed six more matchsticks on to the large pile between them.

'You're bluffing,' accused Peter.

'Am I?' Winston's grin gave nothing away.

'I'll see you.'

'Of course, you'll see me. I'm only a metre away.'

'I'll see your *cards*!'

Peter threw some matchsticks on to the pile, convinced that he had a better hand than Winston. But he did not. Winston put down his five cards and showed his three aces. Peter winced. All that he had was a pair of kings. He'd lost again.

'Another game?' offered Winston.

'No, thanks,' said Peter, dropping the last few matchsticks on to the pile. 'I'm no match for you tonight.'

Winston laughed at the pun and shuffled the cards.

'I had a good run, Peter, that's all.'

'You had Lady Luck on your shoulder.'

This was not strictly true. Winston had something on his shoulder – or just behind it, anyway. But it was not Lady Luck.

It was Slimer.

'Glug-glug-glug.'

Slimer was the green ghostie who slimed Peter on his

first assignment, and the memory could still enrage the Ghostbuster. The two were now friends, however, because Slimer was like a pet. He was a house-trained ghost. Up to a point.

'Glug-glug-glug.'

Slimer was a huge blob of ectoplasm. He had large eyes, large hands and even larger mouth and teeth. The largest thing of all was his appetite. He was always hungry and could not stop eating. That was why he was hovering behind Winston's shoulder during the card game. Slimer was not interested in poker.

He was fascinated by the block of Hershey chocolate that lay open on the table. Peter nibbled at it as he played but there was still a piece left. Slimer's mouth watered as he gazed at it.

'Glug-glug-glug.'

'*No*, Slimer,' said Peter firmly.

'Sch-lurrp!'

'Chocolate is bad for your teeth.'

Peter slipped the last piece into his own mouth.

Slimer heaved a ghostly sigh.

It was bedtime for all three of them.

Janine Melnitz could not even think of turning in yet. She was working late in the reception area on the ground floor. Janine always worked late. It was one of the reasons they employed her. She was the most efficient and conscientious secretary they could have found.

Tall, thin and rather dizzy-looking, Janine was a very cool young lady who never got rattled. She loved her job and her male colleagues but that did not stop her criticising both when she felt like it. Janine had a mind of her own.

'Well done, guys,' she said, as she put a file back in place. 'Another success for the Ghostbusters.'

She had just typed up and filed a report on their last case. No doubt about it. The Ghostbusters gave value for money. They did a job that nobody else in the city would dare to do.

'Ghostbusters are unique!' she said proudly. 'And what's more, there's nobody like us.'

Voices drifted down the stairs.

'Good night, Janine!' called Peter.

'Sweet dreams!' she replied.

'Good night, Janine.'

'See you in the morning, Winston.'

'Glug-glug-glug.'

'Sleep well, Slimer!'

Janine turned back to the filing cabinet and glanced through the long list of successes that it contained. The Ghostbusters had a very good track record. They worked as a team and each member of it made a vital contribution. Janine peered over the top of her glasses and gave a little smile.

'Great stuff, fellas! We're the best!'

She was right.

There was no-one to touch them.

Yet.

New York stayed awake but the Ghostbusters grabbed

some sleep. Snoozing gently in their beds, they all had their dreams. Egon dreamed of inventing a new and more sophisticated ghost-detector. Ray dreamed of building it for him. Peter dreamed of beating Winston at cards. Winston dreamed of getting a whole night's sleep for once.

Slimer dreamed of food.

It was a placid scene.

Four Ghostbusters and an unbusted ghost.

Snoring peacefully through an untroubled night.

BRRING-BRRING!

The alarm bell was a mallet battering at their ears.

BRRING-BRRING! BRRING-BRRING!

They responded instinctively, jumping out of their beds and climbing into their overalls. Still half-asleep, all they could manage were a few grunts of protest.

BRRING-BRRING! BRRING-BRRING! BRRING-BRRING!

Peter Venkman led the way to the firemen's pole that ran from the top to the ground floor. They slid down it at speed with Slimer zipping along behind them.

Janine was waiting with a slip of paper for them. It was the information she had just taken down over the telephone. A desperate call for help. They were needed.

'Big trouble, guys,' said Janine.

'Where?' asked Peter, taking the paper from her.

'Conrad's Factory.'

'Let's go!' shouted Ray.

They ran off to Ecto-1, the Ghostbuster vehicle.

Janine turned to Slimer who was hanging back.

'Aren't you going along for the ride?'

'Gno,' he said, shaking his head.

'I thought Conrad's Factory might appeal to you.'

'Gno-gno.'

'But they make chocolate there.'

'Guzzzzzzzz!'

Slimer twanged. He went after the others in a flash and was just in time to grab hold of the rear fender as the car shot out through the open doors.

They were off to a haunted chocolate factory.

Who knows?

Slimer might get some free samples.

2

Hot Chocolate

Ecto-1 raced through the night at top speed. It shot past slower traffic like a jackrabbit threading its way through a pack of turtles. With its light bar flashing and its siren wailing, it let everyone know that it was coming.

The vehicle was ideal for the needs of the Ghost-busters. It had been an ambulance but Ray Stantz had adapted it for their own special purposes. It was fast, flashy and roomy. When Ray was at the wheel, it handled very well.

'Screeeeeeech!'

They went round a corner then accelerated away towards their destination. A blaze of light up ahead told them that they were getting closer. It was not long before the factory itself came into sight.

'Hot diggety!' said Winston.

'This looks wild,' noted Peter.

'Scientifically, it's very interesting,' added Egon.

'Yeah,' said Ray. 'Who'd want to haunt a chocolate factory?'

Conrad's Factory was enormous. A big, neon-lit sign on top of the building depicted an open box of chocolates. Light was streaming from all the windows and spectral energy was shooting up from its three chimneys.

'It's like nothing we've ever seen before,' said Peter.

A crowd of frightened night-shift workers were shivering outside the main entrance. They had obviously fled their place of work in panic. Police were there in force though none of them dared to go into the building. This crime was beyond them.

Ecto-1 screamed to a halt in front of the factory.

Ray Stantz glanced around at the crowd.

'Boy, are these people scared!'

'They look as if they've seen a ghost,' joked Peter.

'Up there!' said Egon, pointing. 'Those chimneys!'

'Wow!'

The three cement smoke stacks on top of the building now had massive bulges in them. To the sound of maniacal, ghostly laughter, the bulges worked their way up the chimneys until they exploded out of the ends.

'BANG!!!!!'

'Aghhhhhhhhh!'

The crowd yelled and scattered in disarray.

They were under fire.

But it was not bullets they were dodging. Out of the chimneys came a surging stream of chocolates, filling the air all around and falling like hail.

'Bong! Bing! Bung!'

The chocolates bounced off the roof of Ecto-1.

'Man, will you look at this!' said Winston in amazement. 'It's raining chocolate.'

'Better this than raining cats and dogs,' said Peter. He caught a chocolate and tasted it. 'Mm! Soft centres!'

Slimer was in his element.

'Glug-glug-glug!'

While the people ran away from the chocolates, he flew up to greet them. His mouth was wide open and the sweets poured in.

'Munch-munch-munch!'

Slimer's dreams had come true. An unlimited supply of milk chocolate. All he had to do was to eat it.

'Munch-munch-munch! Gobble-gobble-gobble.'

But his greed got the better of him. He swallowed so many chocolates that his stomach became as heavy as lead and he dropped to the ground with a thud.

The Ghostbusters, meanwhile, jumped out of their car.

Egon aimed his PKE meter at the building. It was a device of his own invention for measuring the Psycho-Kinetic Energy that was generated by ghosts.

He got a positive reading and frowned.

'There's a definite PKE source inside,' he said. 'Multiple entities. This could be more dangerous than it looks.'

Peter Venkman caught another chocolate and ate it.

'It may be dangerous but it sure tastes good.'

Ray Stantz was excited by the prospect that lay ahead.

'This is a unique scientific opportunity here!' he asserted. 'Let's go!'

Throwing caution to the winds, Ray led the way forward.

As the Ghostbusters marched past the terrified workers, weird cries and cacklings came from inside the building.

'Wheeeeeeeeeeeee!'

'Hoooooooooooooowl!'

'Yeeeeeaaaaaaaaaah!'

With their Proton Guns at the ready, the Ghostbusters went into the building. It was time to track down their quarry.

Inside the factory was a vast room filled with machinery, cooking vats and a maze of conveyor belts. All of it was running amok with a vengeance. The machinery was vibrating madly, the cooking vats were bubbling furiously and the conveyor belts were zipping along so rapidly that chocolates were hurled everywhere.

In the middle of it all were three ghost monsters.

'Urrrrrrrrrrrrrrrr!'

'Geeeeeeeeeeeeeeee!'

'Zaaaaaaaaaaaaaaaa!'

They were hideous, deformed creatures. Slug was the shortest and oldest of them. An ugly, squat, sour-faced red demon, he was helping to create havoc at the

factory. Slug was the Papa ghost and the others took their cue from him.

Snarg was the Mama ghost, an eerie, pinky-blue spirit with long skinny arms and legs that twisted all over the place. Her skull-like head had wild eyes and giant teeth. Her curly mop of hair was unkempt.

Zonk was the biggest of the three. He was their overgrown son, a warty, pig-snouted, pear-shaped, hairy-tufted beast with a nappie that was held in place by a large safety pin. He sat up on his hind legs like a kangaroo and sniggered.

'Yug-yug-yug-yug-yug-yug-yug-yug!'

The Ghostbusters surveyed the chaotic scene.

'What a mess!' said Peter. 'Reminds me of a college party I went to once.'

'Who's behind it all?' asked Winston.

Egon held up his PKE meter to take a reading.

'We have three Class 5, full torso apparitions,' he said.

'Astonishing!' exclaimed Ray. 'But what bizarre, warped dimension do you think they came from?'

'Possibly New Jersey,' came the dead-pan reply.

'I like it!' said Winston with a laugh.

New Yorkers liked to have a joke at the expense of their neighbours in New Jersey. But Egon was not joking this time. He was very serious. He looked around for the ghosts.

'They could be a real handful,' he warned.

'Then let's go get 'em,' suggested Peter. 'Before all this chocolate makes me come out in spots.'

The Ghostbusters moved forward through the machines with their guns in their hands. Maniacal laughter continued to echo around the place. Then Slug spotted the newcomers and cut short the merriment by elbowing his two companions in the ribs.

'Shuddup!'

'Yeah, Pa,' said Zonk.

'What's up?' croaked Snarg.

They floated in mid-air. Slug pointed to their visitors.

'Down there. Mortals!'

Zonk gave a throaty chuckle of contempt.

'Boy, are they dumb-lookin'!'

The Ghostbusters spotted the trio of monsters. Peter tried to sound friendly as he stepped towards them.

'All right, you party animals,' he said pleasantly. 'It's clean-up time.'

'Listen to him!' said Zonk with a crazy snigger.

'Shuddup!' ordered Slug, punching him.

'Sorry, Pa.'

'I've got a plan.'

'Tell us what it is, Slug,' said Snarg.

The three of them went into a huddle like players in a game of American football. Zonk and Snarg hooted with joy when they heard the plan. Slug gave them the command.

'Right, let's go for it!'

As the Ghostbusters advanced on them, the three monsters flashed across to one of the machines and dived inside a large funnel. Egon, Winston, Ray and

Peter closed in quickly. They felt that they had their prey cornered.

Winston put his face close to the funnel.

'Okay, okay, we know you're in there.'

'So come on out with your claws up!' shouted Peter.

'Don't make us get tough!' warned Winston.

He got his answer at once.

'Whooooooooooosh!'

A wave of chocolate syrup erupted from the funnel and covered his face completely. A jet of whipped cream followed and it was topped off with four cherries. Winston looked like a sundae.

Peter could not stifle his amusement.

'You look good enough to eat, Winston.'

'I don't feel it, man.'

The ghosts had reappeared to shake with mad laughter.

'They think it's great fun,' said Ray.

'Yeah,' agreed Winston. 'I don't believe they're taking us seriously.'

'Activate Proton Guns,' said Egon.

'Take *this*!' yelled Peter.

A beam of energy shot from his particle thrower. It was enough to make the ghosts stop laughing and make a run for it. Chased by the Ghostbusters, they tore around the factory in search of a hiding place. They came to a long, thin pipe with a narrow opening at the end. Slug went into it at speed.

'Zoooooooop!'

Zonk went after him but he was too fat to get in. His

head and shoulders vanished but the rest of him was hanging out. Snarg jumped up and down on his nappie to force him in through the aperture.

'Get in!' she snarled. 'Go on! Hurry up!'

With a final kick, she forced him into the pipe and went in after him. All three were now inside the machinery.

The Ghostbusters studied the escape route.

'They won't get very far!' promised Egon.

'I'll get the trap ready,' said Ray.

He took out his portable ghost trap, a shoebox-sized container unit which was used to house captured ghosts until they could be deposited in the main containment unit back at the headquarters. Ray pressed a button to open the trap.

'Give 'em hell, Egon!'

'They asked for it!'

Egon fired his Proton Gun into the end of the pipe and its beams snaked their way through the machinery. Everything was now shuddering violently and chocolate was pouring out like a waterfall. But Egon kept up the blast. The particles reached the ghosts and they howled in horror.

'Lemme go!'

'Take your lousy hands off me!'

'We was only having fun!'

But their fun was well and truly over.

Slug, Snarg and Zonk were sucked back through the endless twists and turns of the piping. They came out of the opening in a whirlwind of bright light and went straight into the trap.

27

'Zunk! Zunk! Zunk!'

'One, two, three!' cried Ray in triumph, closing the trap.

Everything began to slow down. The machinery stopped, the vats cooled off and the conveyor belts sighed to a halt. The factory was under a layer of chocolate but the ghost party was at last at an end.

Egon used his PKE meter to check for more spirits.

'The place is clean,' he announced.

Winston lifted his boots up with difficulty. The soles were stuck by toffee-like strands to the chocolate-covered floor.

'Clean? Well, yes . . . and no!'

Ray Stantz held the trap up with a broad grin.

'These ghosties won't be any more trouble.'

But they would.

A *lot* more trouble.

The fun had only just started!

3

Slimer's Blow-out

Another mission had been accomplished. The Ghost-busters had done it again. It was almost dawn as they emerged from the main entrance of the factory. The crowd watched nervously.

Ray Stantz held up the ghost trap from which smoke curled.

'It's all over, folks!' he announced. 'We got 'em.'

'Like taking candy from a ghoulie!' said Winston.

'All part of the service,' added Peter.

Sighs of relief went up from the crowd then applause broke out. The Ghostbusters acknowledged their fans with a wave. A television crew moved in to get an interview. Someone thrust a microphone under their noses.

'How was it, Ghostbusters?' asked the interviewer.

'Scientifically, it was intriguing,' said Egon.

'Otherwise, it was rough in there,' explained Peter.

'Yeah,' said Ray, 'they gave us a good fight.'

A big, balding, well-dressed man pushed his way forward.

'Hi, Ghostbusters. You were terrific!'

'Thanks,' said Peter.

'My name is Conrad,' said the man.

'Whaddya know?' observed Ray. 'Same name as the factory.'

'It's *my* factory.'

'That's great chocolate you make, Mr Conrad,' noted Winston.

'I'm glad you think so,' said the man, beaming at them, 'Because I want to give you some of it as a token of my undying appreciation. Gentlemen, I can't thank you enough.'

He handed over some enormous heart-shaped boxes.

'These are for you,' continued the factory owner. 'A year's supply of my finest chocolates.'

'Gee, that's fantastic!' said Ray.

'Extremely generous of you,' agreed Egon.

'You're a big-hearted man, Mr Conrad,' joked Peter.

Winston sniffed the chocolates and grinned.

'How sweet it is!' he said.

Slimer watched it all with eyes like saucers.

'Glug-glug-glug!'

All those lovely, luscious, lip-licking chocolates.

The temptation was irresistible.

After a long and tiring night, the Ghostbusters drove back to their headquarters at a slower pace. The doors

of the fire station swung open as they approached. Ecto-1 turned in and came to a halt. Its rear door was half-open and tied down with rope to hold in the giant chocolate boxes.

'Let's give Janine a surprise,' suggested Egon.

'Sure,' said the others.

They began to untie the rope.

Janine, meanwhile, was sitting at her desk. She started work at dawn and she was now busy typing away. Janine chewed gum as usual. Beside her was a steaming cup of morning coffee and she took an occasional sip from it.

The Ghostbusters came up rather wearily.

'Hi, Janine.'

'Good morning, Janine.'

'We're back, Janine.'

She did not look up from her typewriter.

'Hi, guys,' she said.

The others nudged Egon who stepped forward with one of the heart-shaped boxes. He cleared his throat and spoke bashfully.

'Er, Janine . . . we brought you a little surprise.'

She looked up and her glasses almost fell off her nose.

'Aww, Egon! How sweet!'

Janine took the box from him and lifted off the lid. Her smile of pleasure turned to a frown. She suspected a practical joke and glared angrily at Egon.

'You're right. I *am* surprised!'

'Don't you *like* chocolates?' he asked.

'Sure – when I get them.'

She thrust the box back at him. It was completely empty.

'Hey, what's going on?' said Egon, quite baffled.

'Is this some gag of Mr Conrad's?' wondered Ray.

Janine took the lids off the other boxes and stood over them with her hands on her hips. She was fuming.

'They're all empty, guys.'

'But *how*?' said the mystified Egon.

'Here's the explanation,' she said.

'Where?'

'Take a look in this last box.'

It was the biggest and deepest of the boxes. As the four Ghostbusters peered in over the rim, they saw only too clearly what had happened. Slimer was dozing quietly in the box. He had the contented look of some-one who has just enjoyed the meal of a lifetime. A happy smile played on his chocolate-covered lips.

'He never did!' gasped Egon in disbelief.

'A year's supply!' moaned Winston.

'In one go!' wailed Ray.

'The glutton!' howled Peter.

Slimer dozed peacefully on. His monster meal had turned him into the shape of a beach ball. He touched his round stomach.

'Burp!'

The four Ghostbusters yelled in unison.

'SLIMERRRRRRR!!!!'

Slimer flailed awake. He was so shocked that he jumped into Peter's arms and slimed him. Peter passed

him on to Winston, who got the same treatment. It was Egon's turn next as Slimer was dumped on him then he threw the ghost on to Ray.

'Splop!'

'Yagh! I've been slimed!' cried Ray.

Janine looked on with a sigh. Her suspicions had been wrong.

'Sorry, guys,' she apologised. 'I should've known.'

Slimer now hovered nervously in mid-air.

Peter Venkman grabbed his Proton Gun.

'Stand back, everybody!' he ordered. 'I'm gonna blast him. This time I'm really gonna –'

'Whoa!' said Ray, stepping between him and the ghost. 'Take it easy, Peter. I'll discipline Slimer.'

'It won't work, Ray.'

'Leave it to me.'

Ray stepped in closer to Slimer who gave him an apologetic grin. The Ghostbuster's face was stern. He wagged a finger.

'For shame, Slimer! You've been a naughty ghostie!'

'Naughty!' echoed Peter with disgust. '*Naughty*! Come on, Ray, he's been a major pain.' He turned on the ghost. 'One more mess-up, Slimer, and you're history! Got it?'

'Oo! Ah! Ooo!' whimpered Slimer.

'This is your last warning!'

'Oo!'

Egon yawned then headed for the stairs.

'Hold all our calls, Janine,' he said.

'Yeah,' said Winston. 'We're gonna hit the sheets.'

'It's been a rough night,' added Peter.

The three of them went upstairs while Ray went downstairs.

Janine waved a hand dismissively.

'I'll handle it, guys. Piece of cake.'

At the mention of food, Slimer's interest quickened.

'Cake-cake-cake!'

He began to search her desk, lifting up all the papers.

'It was a figure of speech, Slimer!' she shouted.

He collapsed with disappointment.

'Schl-urpp!'

Ray Stantz had hurried down to the basement with his smoking ghost-trap. The huge containment system had been designed by Egon and built out of the strongest steel. Ghosts were deposited in the main unit and held behind an iron grid.

'Okay, you Class Fives!' said Ray amiably. 'Time to put you into cold storage.'

He opened a metal door in the unit and a big green light started to blink red. Ray inserted the trap. Then he slammed the drawer shut and twisted the handle. There was a long hiss, like the sound of an airlock de-pressurising. Ray yanked a lever and the red light reverted to green again.

'There you are, guys. Safe and sound!'

But not for long.

These ghosts would not stay put so easily.

Up in the dormitory, thick curtains kept out the morning

light. The four Ghostbusters slept heavily in their beds. Peter was on his hands and knees. Winston was on his stomach with a pillow over his head. Egon still held the book he was reading when he dropped off. And Ray cuddled his toy Stay Puft, the flabby ghost who was part of their logo. A chorus of snores went up.

Slimer hovered in mid-air with his head on a pillow. He was not counting sheep. He was counting delicious items of food as they leaped over a stile. Hamburgers, doughnuts, eclairs, ice creams and many other temptations kept coming but somehow he could not get his hands on them. Slimer became so hungry that he began to gnaw at his pillow, eventually swallowing the whole thing.

'Glump-glump-glump!'

He froze in mid-chew. This was not real food.

Slimer came awake with a series of sneezes that sent feathers all over the room. He hid from the snowstorm behind the curtains and peeped out in fear. But the Ghostbusters were not roused. They were far too exhausted.

Slimer's stomach began to grumble noisily.

'Shhhhhhhhhh!' he told it.

But his stomach only grumbled more loudly.

He had to get something to eat. Making sure that the others were still asleep, he zipped out of the dormitory and went downstairs to the kitchen.

A large, full refrigerator beckoned. He caught hold of the handle and pulled but he could not budge it.

'Glug-glug-glug!'

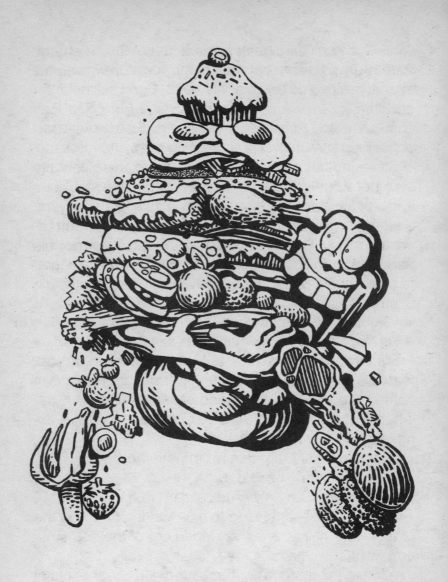

He tried again and gave a much harder tug. The door opened this time — but with such force that he was thrown backwards against the wall.

'Bang!'

Slimer quickly picked himself up and raided the refrigerator. His arms were soon piled high with food and he chuckled merrily to himself. He would have another slap-up meal.

'Bump, bump!'

Slimer stopped in his tracks. Above his head, he heard the sound of footsteps. One of the Ghostbusters must have been awakened by the bang from the kitchen. He was coming down to see what was going on.

Slimer began to shake all over. He would be caught red-handed. Peter had given him a last warning.

He had to hide somewhere. Quickly.

Slimer shot off down to the basement. It was a fatal move.

Without realising it, he would cause a disaster.

4

Greedy Ghosts

Winston Zeddmore heard the noise in the kitchen and got out of bed to investigate. Since the others were fast asleep, he took the responsibility upon himself. Stepping into his slippers, he made his way downstairs. The kitchen was empty. He searched the rest of the first floor but there was nobody about.

Winston shrugged his shoulders and yawned.

'I guess I must've dreamed it!'

Down in the basement, Slimer was hovering in mid-air with the food held precariously in his arms. He was still trembling at the thought of the danger he was in. Suddenly, he lost his grip on the food and it went cascading down to the floor.

'Crash! Bang! Wallop!'

Winston heard the noise clearly up on the first floor.

'Oo! Aah! Ooo!' squealed Slimer.

He flew down and gathered up the items of food as quickly as he could. There was no time to lose. He could hear heavy footsteps coming towards the basement.

The door opened and the tall figure of Winston entered.

'Who's down there?' he asked.

No reply. Winston was at the top of the steel steps that led down into the basement. He did not see the small figure of Slimer hovering directly beneath his feet.

'Is anyone there?' called Winston.

Still no reply. He looked around then shrugged again.

'Funny! Could've sworn I heard something.'

He went out and closed the basement door behind him.

Slimer let out a long, loud sigh of relief.

'Wheeeeeeeeeeeew!'

Still clutching his armload of food, he slid gratefully down the wall of the basement, leaving a trail of ecto-plasm behind him. When he came to the main control switch, he slid over it and pulled it downwards with a clunk. Slimer finished up sitting on the floor with the food before him.

Nothing else mattered. He ate it hungrily.

'Chomp! Chomp! Guzz-guzz!'

He was so involved in what he was doing that he did not see the green light on the containment system turn to red. Slimer had accidentally switched off the unit and it began to react at once. There was a build-up of thermal heat and puffs of steam escaped from the machine. Weird noises came from within and the whole system rocked slightly.

'Chomp! Chomp! Schl-urpp! Schl-urpp!'

He gorged himself on the food. When the banquet was over, he licked his fingers then looked up. Something was wrong.

'Grind! Clank! Hiss!'

The containment system was throbbing violently and steam was hissing out everywhere. The weird noises had got much weirder and there was now an acrid smell.

Slimer went spinning into a panic.

'Goooooaaaaah!'

Retracing his slime-trail up the wall, he came to the main switch and heaved on it. But it was too stiff for him to move. He glanced over his shoulder and saw the unit pulsing with vigour. It could explode at any moment.

Peter Venkman's warning echoed in his ears.

'One more mess-up, Slimer, and you're history!'

They would bust him. He was scared to death.

It put extra strength into his arms as he grappled with the switch again. He pushed up with all his might and – with a superhuman effort – managed to get it in the 'On' position. Power returned at once and coursed through the unit. It stopped hissing and vibrating. The smell vanished. The whole system calmed down.

Another sigh of relief came out of Slimer.

'Wheeeeeew!'

He had saved himself. More important, he had saved the unit. He was confident that he had made amends for his terrible mistake. Slimer did not know that he was too late.

The damage had already been done.

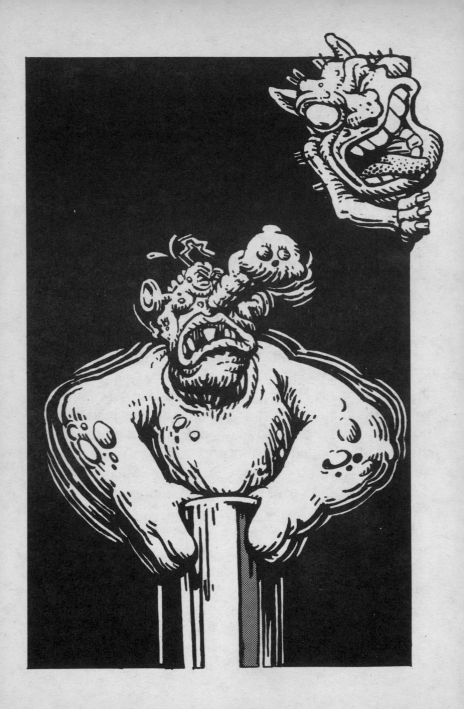

Slug, Snarg and Zonk had been forced through a series of pipes and chambers when the unit was switched off. By the time its energy came on again, they had escaped. The three of them got into the ventilation system and made their way up to the roof of Ghostbuster headquarters. They came out one by one.

'Pop!'

Slug stretched himself after his captivity.

'Boy, was it cramped in there!'

'Pop!'

Snarg jumped out to join him.

'We'll never stay at *that* hotel again,' she promised.

The two of them balanced on a large television aerial and waited for their son to emerge. But Zonk was in difficulties.

'Urgggggggg!'

His head and shoulders came out. The rest was stuck.

The ill-tempered Slug became very impatient.

'Move it, Zonk!' he said harshly. 'We're waitin' on you and I don't like waitin'!'

Zonk grunted and his face twisted into a grimace.

'Comin', Pop.'

Straining hard, he came out bulge by painful bulge.

'Urgggg! Argggg!'

Slug turned vengefully upon his wife.

'I told you to put him on a diet!'

'I did,' she explained, 'but he only lost weight from his head.'

Zonk's massive body was almost out now. It took one

45

more grunt and two more heaves. He came out like a barrage balloon.

'Pop!'

'Made it!' said Zonk in delight.

He jumped up on to the other side of the television aerial. Since he was heavier than the combined weight of his parents, the aerial bent over at a crazy angle and hung out over the busy street.

Zonk gave his stupid, gap-toothed grin.

'Here I am, Pop.'

'Quit slouchin'!' said Slug. 'And comb your hair.'

'Okay.'

Zonk whipped out a comb and started to comb the two long strands of hair in the middle of his bald head. The hair was soon standing on end. He put the comb away.

Snarg snuggled up to her angry husband.

'Now whadda we do, dear?'

Slug let out a roar of uncontrolled fury.

'I'll tell ya what we do!'

'What, Pop?' said Zonk with interest.

'We get even with those stupid Ghostbusters!'

'Yeah!' agreed Zonk, chuckling. 'Get even!'

There was a long pause. Zonk was now bewildered.

'But *how*, Pop?' he asked.

'Watch.'

Slug elbowed Snarg so that she would follow suit. Then he caught hold of the back of his head and pulled it forward like a mask. From being a hideous ghost, he turned into an ugly human being. Snarg underwent a similar transformation. Changing her face, she became a tall, rather snooty lady with rinsed hair.

Their disguise was perfect, Zonk remained in his monster form and scratched his head in wonderment.

'I still don't see,' he admitted.

'We're gonna run those gum-heads right outta business!' said Slug with a sneer. 'Get it now?'

'No, Pop.'

'We're gonna haunt 'em!'

Slug pulled such a frightening face that Zonk jumped off the aerial and on to the roof. With his weight no longer holding it down, the aerial was like a catapult that had just been released. Snarg clung on but Slug was shot through the air at speed. His cry of rage faded as he flew over the rooftops.

'Idiooooooooooooot!'

'Sorry, Pop!' he called.

'C'mon, son,' said his mother. 'Let's go.'

'Where, Mom?'

'Where those Ghostbusters will least expect us.'

They buzzed off across the sky in search of Slug.

It was time to get their own back.

The Ghostbusters were still snoring gently in their beds. Daylight was peeping in through the cracks in the curtains. The sound of traffic outside was a distant buzz that did not disturb them.

But the alarm bell did.

BRRING-BRRING! BRRING-BRRING!

They moved by reflex. Jumping out of their bed; they

pulled on their overalls then raced to the fireman's pole. All four of them slid down to the ground floor where Janine was waving a slip of paper at them.

Egon realised he'd been dragged from his slumbers once again.

'I thought I told you to hold all calls, Janine.'

'Yeah, I know,' she said, 'but this is an emergency.'

'Where is it?' he asked.

'The Central Hospital.'

'Hospital!' repeated Winston. 'Who'd want to haunt a hospital?'

'Someone does,' said Janine. 'They've had several sightings of this one ghost and he's causing mayhem.'

'Only one ghost?' said Peter with contempt. 'It doesn't need four of us to handle one of them.'

'This one sounds like something special,' she warned.

'We'd better check it out,' said Ray.

'Yeah,' agreed Winston. 'The sooner we get over there and zap this ghost, the sooner we can get back to bed.'

The Ghostbusters ran to their vehicle and hopped in.

'We'll teach him to wake us up!' promised Peter.

'Sure thing,' added Ray. 'We'll bust him good and proper.'

'A haunted hospital!' mused Egon. 'This could turn out to be a fascinating phenomenon.'

'Not as fascinating as my bed,' said Winston, yawning. 'Let's go and hit him, guys. He's the enemy!'

'Then he'll get what's coming to him!' vowed Peter.

49

Ecto-1 roared through the open door of the fire station and headed for the Central Hospital. The Ghostbusters were all convinced that it was a routine assignment that would be quickly cleared up by their expertise.

They were in for a big surprise.

5

Ghostly Competition

It started in a side-ward. Everything had been quiet and orderly at the hospital until then. A doctor and a nurse were tending a patient. Curtains had been pulled around the bed for privacy.

The doctor put a soothing hand on the patient's arm.

'All you need now is plenty of rest.'

But he was not going to get it.

At that moment, the curtains were hauled back and the big, terrifying face of Zonk poked itself in. His head seemed to blow right up in size and his tongue snaked out menacingly.

'Peek-a-boo!' he shouted.

'Arghhhhhhhhhh!'

Doctor, nurse and patient fled in mortal terror.

'I was only trying to be friendly!' said Zonk.

He took his friendship to other wards and had them in an uproar. Leaping across empty beds, he chased everyone out. Patients who never thought they would

walk again now found themselves sprinting for their lives.

'Cowards!' yelled Zonk. 'Stay and fight!'

He started to wreck the place with playful zest.

Two strange-looking people appeared in the corridor outside. They wore ill-fitting overalls and carried twin vacuum cleaner hoses that were fitted to a large dustbin on wheels. It was festooned with coils of wire and blinking lights.

One of the doctors saw them and charged over.

'Are you the Ghostbusters?' he gasped.

'Sort of,' said Slug with a low cackle.

'That was quick!' said the doctor. 'We only just phoned.'

'Speed is our watchword,' explained Snarg.

'That's right,' said Slug. 'We always get there first.'

The doctor pointed a trembling finger at the doors.

'He's in that ward. Be careful. He's a great, big, ugly monster and he's on the rampage.'

'We'll handle him,' said Snarg calmly.

'He'll be no trouble at all,' assured Slug.

They went through the swing doors and into the ward.

The doctor watched them go with admiration.

They were very brave to face such a foul fiend.

Siren screaming and lights flashing, Ecto-1 came into the car park at the front of the hospital and skidded to a stop. Staff and patients had been herded outside the main entrance. They were gazing up at the building with open-mouthed horror.

53

The Ghostbusters jumped out of their vehicle.

'Take it easy, folks,' called Peter, holding up his hands like a matinée idol waving to fans. 'Have no fear. Dr Venkman and his staff are here.'

'Everything is under control,' said Ray.

'It sure is!' said a female voice.

The lady doctor had just come out of the hospital with Slug and Snarg. They were wheeling the dustbin which was now bulging and steaming. Its lid was firmly clamped on.

The doctor beamed and indicated her two companions.

'Thanks to these wonderful people, the danger is over.'

'We've got the ugly beast right in here,' said Slug.

He banged the dustbin lid for effect.

A cheer of appreciation went up from the crowd.

'Hooray! Hooray!'

The Ghostbusters stared in blank amazement.

'Wait a minute!' said Peter. '*We* were called in on this case.'

'You got here too late,' said Slug with a laugh.

'We did the job for you,' asserted Snarg.

'Hooray!' yelled the crowd, acclaiming their heroes.

Peter and his team exchanged an uncomfortable glance.

Slug and Snarg wheeled the dustbin across to a large van and loaded it into the rear. They slammed the door shut and were about to get into the cab.

'Hey!' called Peter. 'Who are you people, anyway?'

'We're from Ghosts-R-Us,' said Slug proudly.

'*Who*?' demanded Peter.

'Ghosts-R-Us.'

'You got competition,' explained Snarg with a snigger. 'Better luck next "slime", Ghostbusters. Or should I say – Ghost*busted*?'

They got into their vehicle.

The Ghostbusters studied the logo on the rear doors. It showed a white-sheeted ghost with his tongue sticking out and his thumbs in his ears, as if wagging fingers at his audience. It was a very insolent image.

In large letters was the name: GHOSTS-R-US.

To the sound of maniacal laughter, the van drove off.

The Ghostbusters coughed as they stood in the exhaust fumes.

'Looks like we were beaten to the draw,' admitted Winston.

'How?' asked Peter. 'We're supposed to be the *best*.'

'Not any more,' said Egon sadly.

'They caught us cold,' confessed Ray.

'That's what worried me,' said Egon seriously.

The van tooted its horn and the crowd gave a final cheer.

The Ghostbusters watched with growing concern.

They were baffled.

Janine Melnitz sat behind her desk back at headquarters. Chewing on her gum, she checked through a report she had just typed.

The telephone rang and she picked up the receiver.

'Ghostbusters!' she announced. 'If it goes "boo", we know what to do.'

A woman's voice spoke at the other end of the line.

'Cut out that fuss. Give me Ghosts-R-Us.'

'Ghostbusters-R-Us, ma'am,' said Janine.

'I want the real thing,' insisted the woman.

'We *are* the real thing,' promised Janine. 'We're the original the one-and-only Ghostbusters.'

'Not Ghosts-R-Us?'

'Who are they?'

'Never mind!'

The line went dead and Janine replaced the receiver.

'Zooooooooooom!'

Ecto-1 rocketed home to its garage and came to a halt. Four dejected Ghostbusters came across to her desk. Even Slimer had a despondent look.

'Hey,' said Janine. 'Who is this Ghosts-R-Us? I've had twenty calls for them today.'

'How many for us?' asked Peter.

'None,' she told him.

'Big deal!' he said.

'Who *is* this other company?' she demanded.

'That's what we'd like to know,' said Ray. 'They're stealing all our customers.'

'Are they for real?' she wondered.

'No,' decided Peter. 'I can smell a bogus a mile away and those guys are definitely bogus.'

Egon held up his PKE meter and tapped it.

'Not according to this, Peter,' he said. 'I got a solid

reading from their containment unit. There was definitely a Class 5 phantom in there.'

The Ghostbusters were plunged into gloom.

Winston rallied quickly.

'Come on, guys!' he urged. 'Don't let it get to you. So they sneaked one job from us, that's all. We're still number one. Right?'

'Right!' agreed Ray.

'Top of the heap!' added Peter.

'With superior scientific know-how,' said Egon.

Slimer snorted in eager agreement.

'Schlub-schlub-schlub!'

The telephone rang again and Janine answered it.

'Ghostbusters. We're still number one.'

She listened to a garbled voice and scribbled on her pad.

'Okay,' she said. 'Right. Gotcha.'.

Slamming down the receiver, she tore off the memo for Peter.

'All right, champs! Mid-town hotel. Major disturbance.'

'What are we waiting for!' shouted Peter. 'Let's roll!'

They raced to Ecto-1 and dived straight in.

Ray Stantz gunned the engine and gave a pledge.

'This time nobody beats the Ghostbusters!'

The vehicle went out through the open doors as if it had jet engines under its bonnet. It fairly flew along.

They were determined to get there first.

The hotel was an old, twelve-storey building in the

mid-town area. It had an ornate design and was in good decorative order. The place was dark except for a mysterious momentary brilliance that appeared in all the windows of the individual floors, one floor at a time. Each different random act of illumination was accompanied by a deep bass-like electrical sound. It was totally bizarre.

Hysteria surrounded the hotel. Police barricades held back an anxious crowd who looked up at the lighting display with horror. Their faces were caught in the stroboscopic effect.

Ecto-1 stopped dead in front of the hotel.

The Ghostbusters took stock of the situation.

'Uh, oh!' said Winston. 'This looks bad.'

'It is bad,' endorsed Egon, staring at his flashing meter. 'And getting worse.'

'What's causing that light and sound?' asked Ray.

'Let's go find out,' suggested Peter.

They jumped out of the car and headed towards the building. They were bathed in the blinking glare which got faster and faster.

'Stand back, folks!' warned Ray.

A policeman blocked their way. Peter waved him aside.

'Official business!' said Peter. 'We're scientists.'

'Glad to see you, fellas!' welcomed the cop. 'That place has gone bananas!'

'We'll soon sort it out,' said Peter confidently.

He led the way purposefully towards the main entrance.

Then the light and the music halted abruptly.

So did the Ghostbusters.

'What's going on?' asked Peter in amazement.

'Oh, no!' said Ray. 'Look up there!'

They gazed up at a window on one of the upper floors.

The faces of Slug and Snarg beamed out at them.

'Go home, Ghostbusters,' called Slug. 'This is a wrap.'

'Thanks to Ghosts-R-Us!' said Snarg.

Their mocking laughter came swooping down from above.

'Who *are* you guys?' demanded Peter.

'This was *our* call!' protested Ray.

'You shouldn't be so slow to answer it,' said Slug.

The two figures withdrew from the window and the hotel began to light up again. When the bottom floors blazed with light, Slug and Snarg came out with their steaming, bulging cannister on its wobbly wheels.

'We got the ghost!' Slug yelled to the crowd. 'It's fine now, ladies and gentlemen. No problem.'

A rousing cheer went up for their success.

The Ghostbusters glared in slack-jawed disbelief.

'How'd you get here before us?' asked Winston.

'Because we're Numero Uno,' said Slug, holding up an index finger to make his point. 'We're Number One!'

'And you aren't!' reinforced Snarg nastily.

The crowd went delirious as they cheered their new heroes.

'Ghosts-R-Us!' they chanted, 'Ghosts-R-Us!'

Television cameras closed in on Slug and Snarg.

Interviewers thrust microphones at them and plied them with questions. They were getting national publicity for their latest triumph.

The Ghostbusters were even more cast down.

'You know,' said Peter. 'There's something very familiar about those guys.'

'Something very ugly about them, too,' noted Winston.

Egon took a realistic view and it was depressing.

'Whoever they are, they're putting us right out of business.'

It could mean the end of the Ghostbusters.

6

Slimer Owns Up

When they finished their television interviews, Slug and Snarg loaded the dustbin into the back of their van and drove away. They were given a tumultuous send-off by the crowd. The fame of Ghosts-R-Us was sealed.

Inside the van, there was great mirth and hilarity.

'See those dumb Ghostbusters' faces?' said Slug.

'They didn't know what hit them,' replied Snarg.

'We haven't started yet,' promised her husband. 'They asked us who we were.'

'Ghosts-R-Us!'

'That's right,' agreed Slug, pulling off his mask so that his hideous demonic face came back into view. 'We are ghosts. We are us. So – Ghosts-R-Us!'

They sniggered together as they drove along.

The lid suddenly shot up off the dustbin.

'Clang!'

Zonk peeped out then stood up in the bin.

65

'Was I good, Pop?' he asked. 'Was I convincing?'

'Terrifying, son.'

'You put the fear of death into 'em,' said Snarg.

'So what's next?' wondered Zonk.

'We run them out of town,' decided Slug.

'How, Dad?'

'I'll think of a way. We're gonna put those Ghost-busters outta business for good.' He looked critically at Zonk. 'Meanwhile . . .'

'Yeah, Pop?'

'Comb your hair!' snapped the other.

'Sure, sure.'

Zonk took out his comb and attacked the two lone hairs on his otherwise bald skull. They soon stood straight up. He grinned hopefully at his father for approval.

'How's that, Pop?'

'Much better. We gotta keep up appearances now.'

'Yes,' added Snarg. 'We're Ghosts-R-Us!'

Their cackles mingled joyfully together.

There was no laughter in Ecto-1 as it limped towards home. Ray Stantz drove slowly and the others sat there in sullen silence. They had been stunned by what had happened. Even Slimer was subdued for once. He actually forgot that he was hungry.

Janine's voice suddenly cut in on the radio.

'Spook Central calling Ecto-1!'

Peter snatched the microphone from the dashboard.

'Go ahead, Janine,' he ordered.

'Better hurry back, guys,' suggested the secretary. 'There's something very freaky going on here.'

'What is it?' asked Peter.

'That's the problem. I'm not sure.'

'Hold on, Janine. We're on our way.'

The sluggish vehicle picked up speed at once. Cornering on two wheels, it zoomed away until it reached the fire station. It shuddered to a halt and they leaped out to run across the secretary's desk. For once, she was not there.

'Janine!' they called in unison.

'Down here!' she answered from the basement.

They hurried on down there to join her. Janine was holding a clipboard and standing in front of the containment unit. Her face was puckered into a frown of anxiety.

'What's wrong?' said Winston.

'Are you okay?' asked Egon, worried for her.

'Me?' she said, flattered by his concern. 'Sure, Egon. I'm fine. The problem is with the unit here.'

'In what way?' pressed Egon.

'I was taking some routine readings and the spectral count doesn't jibe.'

The Ghostbusters reacted with a chorus of alarm.

'WHAT!!!!'

Janine pointed to the odometer-like counter on the unit.

'This whatchamadoodle says we're three ghosts short.'

'That's impossible!' argued Ray.

67

'Nothing can escape that system unless it's shut down,' explained Egon.

Slimer's eyes began to rotate as he realised what must have happened. He wished that he could somehow vanish altogether.

'Oo! Ah! Ooo!'

Peter Venkman thought hard for a moment then he snapped his fingers. One puzzle was solved.

'Hey, wait a minute!' he said. 'That's who those Ghosts-R-Us goons looked like. The three Class Fives we nailed this morning.'

'You're right!' agreed Winston. 'Who could forget ugly mugs like that?'

'But how did they escape?' asked a perplexed Ray.

'Somebody must have shut down the containment unit!' decided Egon. 'It's the only way it could have happened.'

'But who would do such a stupid thing?' asked Peter.

A moaning sound came from the corner of the room.

Slimer was pretending not to be there but his guilt was giving him away. He groaned as he saw what he had done. Thanks to him, the Ghostbusters might be thrown out of work.

'Oo! Ah! Ooo!'

All five of them turned on him as one.

'SLIMERRRRRRRR!!!!'

'Gub-gub?' said Slimer, pointing to himself.

'Yeah – *you*!' emphasised Peter.

'Ga-Ga-Ga-Ga-Ga-Ga-Ga-Ga!' sobbed Slimer.'

'I knew I should have blasted him!' roared Peter.

'Ga-Ga-Ga-Ga-Ga-Ga-Ga!'

Slimer cried onto Ray's shoulder and slimed it.

'Okay, okay,' said Ray. 'We forgive you, Slimer.'

'Just tell us how it happened,' urged Egon.

Slimer did not get the chance. The telephone rang. Janine reached for the basement extension and took the call. She nodded eagerly throughout.

'Don't worry, sir. They're on their way.'

'More work for us?' asked Peter as his hopes rose.

'At the harbour,' she said. 'An ocean-going liner.'

'All aboard!' shouted Peter.

And away they went.

The crowd at the quayside were looking warily at the huge liner as if it were on the point of exploding. A weird glow kept appearing at each of the portholes. Columns of spectral energy shot up from the massive funnels. The strange music from the hotel was repeated in deep bass chords. It was unnerving.

Dockside security men held back the crowd. They were relieved when Ecto-1 came wailing into view. As the vehicle stopped, the four Ghostbusters got out to assess the situation.

'Floating ghosts!' observed Egon. 'Utterly fascinating.'

'What does the meter say?' asked Peter.

'Class 5,' observed Egon.

'It's *them*. I'm sure.' Peter was jubilant.

'Let's trap them for good this time,' said Ray.

They went up the gang plank and on to the ship.

As soon as they were aboard, it began to list from side to side as if pushed by some invisible hand. They went down some narrow steps and followed the light. The problem was that it kept appearing in different cabins as if by magic.

Winston held his Proton Gun ready while the others called out the number of the cabin in which the weird light shone.

'Number fifteen!'

'No, number seventeen!'

'It's number nineteen now!'

'No, it isn't. Number twenty-one!'

'Slow it down!' yelled Winston. 'I can't get a shot in at this rate. There it is – number twenty-three!'

But even as he opened the cabin door, the light vanished and reappeared next door. It was like a game of hide-and-seek and the Ghostbusters were at a strong disadvantage. Their prey was always one step ahead of them.

When they came down to the cabins on the lower deck, a strange sight greeted them. There was a fire hose coiled up on the wall. To the sound of Eastern music, it began to unwind like a snake. It danced in front of them until they were mesmerised. Then its nozzle was directed right at them.

'Splaaaaaaaash!'

They were drenched by a stream of cold water.

'Hey!' yelled Peter.

'It's not our bath night!' complained Winston.

A distinctive grunting chuckle rang out nearby.

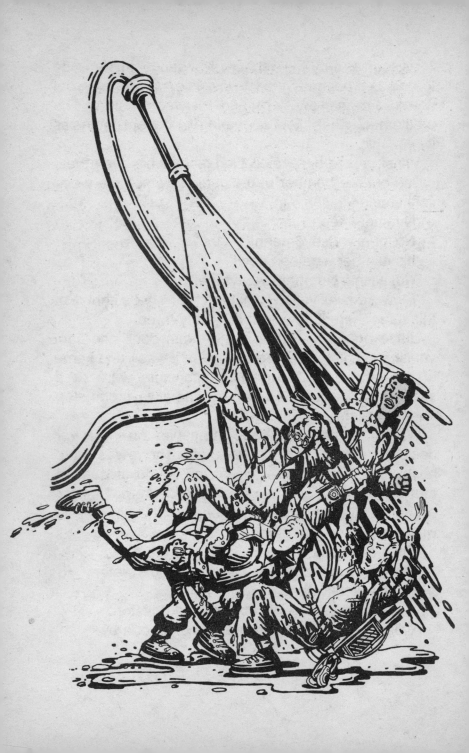

'Clean up your act, Ghostbusters,' said Zonk.

They spun round in time to see him flit upstairs.

'After him!' shouted Ray.

'I'll reduce him to a frazzle,' said Peter, waving his gun.

'He's one of those Class Fives!' insisted Egon.

They raced up the stairs as fast as they could but Zonk was moving with great speed. When they came out on the main deck, the monster seemed to have disappeared. A voice then came out of the foghorn.

'Come and get me!'

It was Zonk. They rushed across to the large foghorn and peered into the end. They could see nothing inside.

'We got you cornered!' warned Peter.

'Give up while you gotta chance!' advised Ray.

'There's no escape this time!' said Winston.

The foghorn gave a long, deafening blast.

'Blaaaaaaaaaaaaaaaaaaaaa!'

They jumped back and covered their ears with their hands.

'Okay,' decided Egon. 'Let's give him all we got!'

Egon, Peter and Winston aimed their particle throwers into the foghorn. Ray stood by with the ghost-trap. The three men fired together. Their energy beams went right down the tube. Nothing could survive that onslaught. They'd got him.

Loud cheers suddenly went up from the quayside.

'Hooray! Hooray!'

'What's that noise?' wondered Egon.

'Let's get this ghostie first,' suggested Peter, 'then we can go take a look.'

'There *is* no ghostie,' sighed Winston.

They put their Proton Guns aside and peeped into the smoking ruin of the foghorn. There was nothing inside. Zonk had somehow eluded them again.

'Hooray! Hooray!'

They rushed to the side of the ship and looked over. Down on the quayside, two familiar figures were getting a rousing welcome and they wheeled their steaming dustbin along.

Ghosts-R-Us had done it again.

'I don't believe it!' said Ray.

'How do those guys *do* it!' gasped Winston.

'We're the best,' admitted Peter. 'But they're even better.'

The Ghostbusters were hurt and mystified.

Their whole future was at risk.

7

A Phantom Call

Basking in the applause, Slug and Snarg drove off in
their van. They had humiliated the Ghostbusters once
again. They sniggered with evil satisfaction. Ghosts-R-
Us was a tremendous success. Slug took all the credit
for thinking up the idea.

'I'm brilliant!' he boasted.

'Yeah,' said Snarg. 'I always knew you had brains.'

'Just as well someone in this family does!'

'I'm not *that* dumb,' she argued.

'You're not – but *he* is!'

Slug banged on the lid of the dustbin with his fist.

'Aouw!'

Zonk surfaced from the dustbin, rubbing the top of his
head.

'That hurt, Pop!'

'Serves you right for not combing your hair.'

'I hate this stupid bin!' moaned Zonk. 'How much
longer do we hafta do this, Pop?'

'One last time, son.'

'Is that all?' said Snarg.

'Yeah,' promised Slug. 'Then the Ghostbusters'll be history!'

He went off into a wild laugh which abrubtly stopped. He clipped Zonk's ear with his hand and bellowed into it.

'Comb your hair!'

The Ghostbusters returned to their headquarters in grim silence. They sat in the reception area and brooded while Janine typed away. Somehow they had to catch up with the three ghosts who had escaped from their containment system. Otherwise, their prospects looked very bleak.

'What else could we do?' said Ray soulfully.

'Instead of ghostbusting, you mean?' asked Winston.

'Yeah.'

'Dunno, Ray. Nuttin', really.'

'Nothing as good as busting ghosts, anyway,' said Peter.

'And nothing as scientifically important,' added Egon.

'There's another thing,' reminded Ray.

'What?' said Winston.

'If this place closes, what happens to Slimer?'

The four Ghostbusters looked around at their pet. Slimer felt very lonely and vulnerable.

'Wheeeee!' he whimpered.

They lapsed back into silence. It was soon broken.

'Ring-ring! Ring-ring!'

Janine snatched up the receiver and spoke into it.

'Ghostbusters here!' she announced. 'And don't you dare ask for Ghosts-R-Us!'

A trembling voice was heard at the other end of the line.

'We need help – fast! This place is haunted.'

'Where exactly are you, sir?' she asked.

Janine wrote down the address on a slip of paper and gave it to Peter. With a hand over the mouthpiece of the telephone, she turned to the Ghostbusters.

'This one's a biggie, guys. An old toy factory in Brooklyn.'

'What about those escaped Class Fives?' said Ray.

'Knowing them, they're probably already there,' said Egon.

'Yeah,' agreed Peter. 'They set this whole thing up.'

'Then let's go bag those turkeys!' urged Winston.

They dashed off to Ecto-1 as fast as they could.

Janine resumed her telephone call.

'Are you still there, sir?' she asked.

'Still here,' moaned the voice. 'And still scared!'

'Help is on the way.'

'Good. The sooner the better.'

'The Ghostbusters will solve your problem, sir.'

'I hope so, lady.'

Janine put down the receiver and smiled.

This time, she felt, the Ghostbusters would come out on top.

Their reputation was at stake.

They would rise to the challenge.

Whoops of mad laughter came from a telephone booth in Brooklyn. Slug, Snarg and Zonk were all crammed inside together. Slug had used a false voice to speak to Janine. He now went back to his own grating rasp.

'She said that help was on the way!' recalled Slug. 'So I told her the sooner the better!'

'Yeah,' said Zonk. 'Sooner!'

'Shuddup!' snarled his father.

Slug hit Zonk's nose hard and it vibrated like a tuning fork.

'What was that for, Pop! I combed my hair.'

'Button your lip as well.' Slug began to smirk again. 'Hey, what about that? They're coming! They're coming!'

'The Ghostbusters are coming!' repeated Snarg.

'Pretty soon, they'll be going as well,' said Slug.

'Going, Pop?' questioned Zonk.

'Yeah – right outta business.'

The three of them burst into peals of wild laughter. The telephone booth rocked violently from side to side as they celebrated their success. Eventually, the booth was torn away from the ground.

'Wreeeeeeench!'

Their feet poked out of the bottom. With the telephone booth wrapped around them like a corset, they scampered happily off through the streets of Brooklyn.

'They're coming! They're coming! They're coming!'

The final battle was now at hand.

Ghostbusters versus Ghosts-R-Us.

It would be a fight to the death.

Ecto-1 burrowed its way through the heavy Manhattan traffic as it headed for Brooklyn Bridge. Seated in the back with Winston and Slimer, Egon reflected on what had happened.

'You gotta hand it to those guys,' he said.

'I'll hand it to 'em,' vowed Ray. 'With my Proton Gun.'

'It's a great concept,' continued Egon. 'Ghosts who pretend to bust ghosts. They haunt a place and then arrive on the scene as the Ghostbusters. No wonder they get there before us.'

'This is their last case,' asserted Peter.

'They'll go in the containment unit to stay,' added Egon.

'Hear that, Slimer?' warned Peter. 'You play with that switch again and *you* end up in the containment unit as well.'

Slimer trembled in the rear of the vehicle.

'Oo! Ah! Ooo!'

Peter Venkman rammed his point home.

'We got enough ghosts to take on as it is,' he said. 'We don't need you to sabotage us. Got it, Slimer? You're supposed to be on *our* side!'

'Glug-glug-glug.'

Slimer was contrite. He would try to do better.

The old toy factory in Brooklyn was immense. Dark and deserted, it was reminiscent of a rusty abandoned airplane hangar. Steel latticework trusses reached high into the recesses of its ceilings. Long chains hung down, swinging and clanking in the breezes that blew through

the broken windows. Water dripped from above, creating dank puddles.

Looming inside the building were massive, rust-covered machines with a menacing air to them. There were holes in the roof and the charred debris showed that there had been a bad fire there at one time. On the cobwebbed assembly lines were the last of the toys, some melted and disfigured, others still in good condition.

Slug, Snarg and Zonk arrived to look around.

They gazed at the scene of devastation. Baby dolls, electric trains, rubber ducks, beach balls, tin drums, toy soldiers and many other things lay in the middle of the wreckage.

The three monsters were dwarfed by the size of the place.

Zonk shivered with apprehension.

'This place is weirrrrrrd!'

'Look who's talkin',' observed Slug sarcastically.

'It gives me the creeps, Pop!'

'Your father knows best, dear,' said Snarg.

'But what're we doin' here, Mom?' he asked.

'Looking up an old friend.'

'Yeah,' added Slug. 'A Class 7 phantom named Turlock. He haunts this dump.'

Zonk gulped and went all colours of the rainbow.

'Class 7!' he cried in horror. 'B-but they're v-very p-powerful, aren't they?'

'Right,' snarled Slug. 'That's why Turlock's gonna make those Ghostbusters run for the next state.'

He nudged Snarg who joined in with his wicked cackle.

Slower to grasp what was going on, Zonk grinned uncertainly.

'Er, this Turlock . . . what'll he do to them, Pop?'

'Everything!'

Slug's cackle grew louder then he grabbed a rope and began to climb down into the deep, black cellar of the building. Zonk watched him go and turned to his mother for reassurance.

'Mom . . .'

'Yeah?'

'Turlock *is* a friend, isn't he?'

'One of the best.'

'So he won't hurt *us*.'

'Not a chance, son. He only eats mortals.'

'That's okay,' said Zonk with relief.

Slug, meanwhile, had picked his way through the rubble in the cellar until he came to a small barred window. It was in the wall of a huge cavern that lay in dark shadow. Holding on to one of the bars, he put his head in and called.

'Hey, Turlock!'

There was no sound from inside the cavern.

'It's me!' he shouted. 'Slug! C'mon out!'

But there was no reply. He became impatient. Grabbing an old piece of iron, he banged it between the bars to make a loud noise. The cavern was like an echo chamber and the sound was amplified many times.

'C'mon, Turlock!' yelled Slug. 'We need ya to do a first-rate hauntin' for us!'

Something stirred deep in the gloom.

'That's better,' said Slug. 'Over here.'

If he had known what would happen next, he would never have dared to bang on the bars like that. He would probably never have dared even to come to Brooklyn.

Big trouble was on its way.

8

A Surprise in Store

Unaware of the danger, Slug leaned in through the bars and chatted familiarly. He still believed his old friend was inside.

'That's it, Turlock. Wake up in there.'

The rustling noises got much louder.

'I want you to do a favour for a pal.'

A low, eerie moan came out of the pitch darkness.

'Whooooooooooooooooo!'

'That's great, Turlock,' complimented Slug, 'but we're not ready for the hauntin' yet.'

The second moan was ten times the volume of the first.

'WHOOOOOOOOOOOOOOOOOOO!'

'Take it easy, old pal!' soothed Slug.

Suddenly, the whole place began to shake and shudder. A fierce wind came up from nowhere and there was a loud hissing.

Slug decided that it was all a joke.

'C'mon, Turlock!' he said. 'Quit kiddin' around!'

He then saw something which took his breath away.

'Crrrrrrrrrrrrrr!' he croaked.

Erupting out of the darkness came a long, thick trunk that shot between the bars of the window and snapped them as if they were matchsticks. At the end of the trunk was a huge, red, glaring eye. It was several times the size of Slug and he cowered before it. The eye regarded him with sullen anger.

This demon was far bigger than Turlock had been.

It was surrounded by curling fog and its voice was a hiss.

'Who are you?' demanded the demon.

'Me? I'm Slug,' stuttered the other.

'I hate slugs!' hissed the voice.

'H-hold on a m-minute! W-where's T-Turlock?'

'Gone!'

'G-Gone?'

'Permanently!'

The eye came closer and the voice grew more menacing.

'This is *my* domain now.'

'Yeah, yeah,' said Slug. 'Anything you say.'

'You disturbed me!'

As the demon lunged at him, Slug let out a howl of fear.

'Arghhhhhhhhhhhh!'

He climbed back up the rope at great speed. Snarg and Zonk were waiting for him but Slug was too frightened to speak. He just kept pointing downwards.

'What's up, Pop?' asked Zonk.

'Is Turlock coming, dear?' said his wife.

'Boy, am I looking forward to meeting him eye to eye.'

The demon's monstrous eye shot up to confront him. Zonk drew back in alarm. He turned to his parents.

'Is this Turlock?'

They shook their heads and backed away.

'So what do we do?'

'Runnnnnnnnnnnnnnnnnnnnn!' yelled Slug.

The three of them turned tail and fled at top speed.

'I'll get you!' hissed the demon.

It moved on foggy tentacles to the middle of the factory where an old machine was standing. Climbing into the machine, the creature used its tentacles to reach out and scoop up some of the toys that lay abandoned on the floor.

The misty tendrils dropped the toys into the top of the machine and then it breathed supernatural life into them to inflate them to many times their normal proportions. Shafts of bright light shone out of the cracks in the steel and there were loud clanking sounds from within. The machine itself was then transformed into part of the creature.

It was gigantic. The body was a massive building block with letters painted on the sides. On its front side was a face that was consumed with rage.

Huge steel legs supported the block. Standing on top of it was a large, brown monkey with a fixed grin on its face. It was holding a pair of cymbals which it clanged together as the creature started to walk.

'Clang-clang! Clang-clang!'
The toy monster was on the move.
It was vast.

The Ghostbusters raced over Brooklyn Bridge in Ecto-1 and took the fastest route to the toy factory. When they came down the street, they went past the building by mistake and had to brake. They reversed for a bit then swung on to the land in front of the factory. The car juddered to a halt.

'What a crumby-looking joint!' observed Ray.

'Full of psychic possibilities,' said Egon.

Peter looked around with a sardonic smile.

'Well, whaddya know?' he said. 'For a change, we're actually the first ones here.'

He spoke too soon.

'Heeeeelp!!'

Screeching at the top of their voices, Slug, Snarg and Zonk came leaping over the fence in front of Ecto-1. They landed on the bonnet of the vehicle and made it rock up and down as they ran over its roof and on down the street. They were obviously very distressed about something.

The Ghostbusters sat there calmly and Peter shrugged.

'Make that the "second ones" here,' he corrected.

He spoke too soon once more.

'CRASHHHHHHHH!'

The demon came walking through the wall, demolishing the brickwork with ease. With long, clanking footsteps, it set off after the fleeing trio of ghosts.

'ROARRRRRRRRR!'

The Ghostbusters blenched at the frightening spectacle.

'Would you believe the "third one's" here?' said Winston.

Slimer let out a squeal of fear and dived into the glove compartment. He had seen more than enough.

Ray Stantz looked after the demon.

'Did you see those eyes?' he said in astonishment. 'That's at least a Class 8 free-roaming vapour.'

Egon consulted his PKE meter.

'Worse,' he confirmed. 'A full magnitude Class 10.'

The arrow on his meter shot out of its dial completely.

'Whatever it is,' said Winston, 'it's about to mash Manhattan into cheese spread.'

'Time to save our city, guys!' announced Peter.

'*How*?' asked Ray.

'We'll figure that out when we get there,' said Peter.

'Hold tight, guys!' warned Ray.

Ecto-1 reversed out into the street, screamed to a halt then set off in pursuit of the toy monster.

It was one of their biggest challenges yet.

Traffic snarled up in the main streets of Brooklyn. Horns sounded and angry voices were raised. But there was no movement at all. Bumper to bumper, the cars were held fast in a jam.

Inside one taxi, a customer lost his temper.

'Get a move on, will ya?' he ordered.

'I'm doin' my best, pal!' replied the driver.

'It ain't good enough.'

'Nobody's movin',' said the driver. 'It's packed solid up in front of me. Yeah, and it's the same behind.'

He glanced in his wing mirror and turned white.

'Holy smoke!'

'What's up?' asked the passenger.

'Duck!'

The driver covered his head with his hands and bent down.

Within seconds, there were three loud thuds on the roof of the taxi as Slug, Snarg and Zonk bounced off. They were hopping from vehicle to vehicle in a mad panic.

There was far worse to come.

'ROARRRRRRRRR!'

The demon had converted its steel legs into a child's bicycle with massive wheels. It was flattening everything in its path, leaving a trail of destruction in its wake. If it continued to freewheel like that, the whole city would be levelled.

Nothing could stop it.

Except the Ghostbusters.

Ecto-1 flashed through Brooklyn at tyre-burning speed with Peter Venkman at the wheel. It zigzagged its way through the burned-out wrecks and mangled remains of other vehicles. The toy monster was easy to follow. It left its wheel-prints everywhere.

'Okay, boys!' declared Peter. 'Round-up time! Winston and I'll ride herd.'

'What about us?' asked Ray from the rear of the car.

'You and Egon head 'em off at the pass in Ecto-2.'

'You got it!' said Ray with enthusiasm.

'Let's go, partner!' said Egon.

They pulled on their special goggles then turned to the scooter-like vehicle that was stored in the rear of Ecto-1. It was a two-seater with its own set of Cadillac tail-fins. Like Ecto-1, it was festooned with lights, gadgets and fancy chrome-work. There were two wheels at the front and one at the back. All of them were thick and knobbly like aircraft tyres.

Ecto-2 had been designed by Egon and built by Ray from an assortment of salvaged odds and ends. The two Ghostbusters were glad of a chance to put their invention to the test. They climbed into their saddles and waited for the signal.

'Okay?' called Peter.

'Ready when you are!' replied Egon.

'Launch!'

A light came on above their heads. Then the tailgate went up and they were jettisoned out of the back. Ecto-2 landed on the road surface with a bump.

Egon pressed a button and wings sprouted.

Ray began to have second thoughts about it all.

'Hey, Egon? Did you ever have those flying lessons?'

'No,' admitted the other.

But that did not stop him pressing the ascent button. With a loud whirring noise, Ecto-2 flew upwards like a

miniature helicopter. The two Ghostbusters were going to take on the might of the toy monster.

They did not realise that they had assistance.

Clinging to the back of their craft was Slimer.

'Glug-glug-glug.'

He was terrified.

But he was also determined to help.

9

Ghost-trapping

Ecto-1 had to slow down as the wreckage ahead thickened but Ecto-2 had no such problems. Soaring up among the skyscrapers, it made light of the obstruction. Egon and Ray were given a bird's-eye view. They could see the devastation all too clearly.

Egon switched on his radio and spoke to Ecto-1.

'Those Class Fives are heading for the river!'

'What about that Class Ten?' asked Peter's voice.

'Right behind 'em.'

'Okay. We'll meet you at the bridge.'

'Check!'

Egon manoeuvred the craft so that it flew in a wide arc towards Brooklyn Bridge. Ray and Slimer held on tight. Ahead of them was the giant figure of the toy monster, crushing all that got in its way. No wonder Slug, Snarg and Zonk were retreating.

Traffic on the bridge was at a standstill.

'Faster!' urged Slug, jumping from roof to roof.

'I'm doing my best, dear!' puffed Snarg just behind him.

'Wait for me!' called the panting Zonk.

Slug shot his son a withering glare over his shoulder. 'Comb your hair!'

'Not now, Pop!!'

They went recklessly on, leaving dents in the roofs of all the vehicles they bounced on. Egon swung Ecto-2 down at the far side of the bridge to lay an ambush.

'We got them covered at this end,' he said into his radio microphone. 'You get 'em if they double back.'

'Leave it to us,' answered Peter's voice.

'Stand by with that ghost-trap,' said Egon.

'It's all ready,' promised Ray, holding it up.

'Good.' Egon checked his watch. 'I'd say we'll rendez-vous with those characters in exactly five seconds.' He began a count-down. 'One-two-three-four-five . . .'

'Zero!' shouted Ray.

Slug and Snarg arrived bang on time. When they saw the trap gaping open for them, they dived from the roof of a taxi and went gratefully in.

'Look out!' called Slug.

'Here we come!' yelled Snarg.

The trap slammed shut behind them. Zonk then appeared.

'Make room for me!' he cried.

Ray pressed the switch to open the trap again.

'Made it!' said Zonk, going headfirst in.

The trap snapped shut once more.

'So much for Ghosts-R-Us!' noted Egon.

'They're the least of our worries,' said Ray.

'ROARRRRRRRRRRRR!'

The toy monster rolled its way threateningly towards them.

'Take us up, Egon!' ordered Ray.

'Don't worry. I will.'

Before the monster could grab them with its telescopic arms, Ecto-2 went up into the sky again and hovered over the bridge. The monster's wheel now converted back to steel legs. It stood among the ruined cars and waved a fist up at the Ghostbusters.

'Let's hit him!' said Ray, lifting his Proton Gun.

'Aim for the monkey!' suggested Egon.

'I'll wipe that grin off his face!'

Ray aimed the particle thrower and fired. The beam of energy shot out and hit the monkey right in the face. But there was an unexpected result.

As the animal was knocked backwards, the lid of the block flew open and up popped a hideous Jack-in-the-box.

'Ya-yak-yak-yak-yak-yak-yak!'

Its grin was even bigger than the monkey's.

'I've got a plan,' said Egon.

'What is it?' asked Ray.

'Lassoo that thing.'

'Check.'

Using a special gun, Ray Stantz fired a coil of rope at the Jack-in-the-box. It went around its neck and tightened.

'We got it!' shouted Egon in triumph.

'No,' wailed Ray. 'It's got *us*.'

The monster's hand reached up to hold the rope then it twirled it around in the air. Egon, Ray and Slimer were helpless. They were spinning around like the wheels of a windmill.

'Great plan, Egon!' said Ray ruefully.

'Hold tight, guys!' advised Egon.

They went faster and faster.

Peter Venkman and Winston Zeddmore, meanwhile, had met a solid wall of traffic. They had to adopt emergency measures.

Winston spoke into the radio microphone.

'We're on our way but the traffic's killing us!'

'Hang on!' warned Peter. 'I know a short cut.'

'You'll never get through this,' said Winston.

'No? Just watch.'

Peter accelerated straight at a wrecked car, giving it a glancing blow on purpose. Ecto-1 was knocked sideways so that it was travelling on two wheels. It was now only half as wide as it had been before and was able to sneak past the traffic on the inside. When it got to the middle of the bridge, it banged back down onto four wheels.

High above them, Ecto-2 was whirring like a Catherine wheel.

'We gotta save them!' said Peter.

'Give that thing a blast together!' urged Winston.

'Okay! Aim for its leg.'

Directing their guns at the massive steel leg, they fired.

'ROARRRRRRRRRR!'

The monster was sufficiently hurt to let go of the rope and send Ecto-2 flying into the air. It came down with a thud on the topmost part of the bridge's superstructure.

The monster, meanwhile, tried to flatten Ecto-1 beneath its huge foot. Peter reversed the vehicle just in time. Still smarting from the wound, the monster now turned its attention back to Ecto-2. Climbing on to the bridge, it began to ascend like an engine of doom.

'Clump! Clump! Clump! Clump!'

There was no means of escape for Egon and Ray.

They had to wait up there while vengeance approached.

'Clump! Clump! Clump! Clump!'

Winston pointed upwards in great alarm.

'They'll be smashed to pieces by that thing!'

'Yeah,' said Peter. 'And you can blame it all on Slimer.'

'I know.'

'If Slimer hadn't messed up, we'd be home in our jammies right now. It's all his fault!'

Perched up on top of the bridge, Slimer heard every word over the two-way radio. He was cut to the quick. Peter was right. It all began when he let the ghosts escape from the containment system.

The words came back to haunt him again.

'. . . blame it all on Slimer . . .'

It was true. He had put his friends' lives in danger.

'. . . if he hadn't messed up . . .'

Slimer accepted responsibility and did something about it. Breathing hard to build up his strength, he bent back and then unleashed himself towards the bridge's inclined suspension cable.

'Slimer! Wait!' warned Egon.

'He'll tread on you like a fly!' said Winston.

But Slimer was unafraid. He knew what he was doing.

The monster got closer and closer.

'Clump! Clump! Clump! Clump!'

Egon had another plan. Pulling out a small device, he flicked a switch on it and a red light came on.

'I've set it for blast-off,' he told Ray. 'When I give the word – jump!'

'I'll be with you.'

Slimer now put his own plan into operation.

He slid down the girder towards the toy monster.

It looked as if he was about to commit a ghostly suicide.

At the last moment, however, he leaped off the girder and floated down through the air. Behind him was a trail of greasy, treacherous slime. The monster's feet slipped on it and he lost his balance completely. He dived towards Egon and Ray.

'Jump!' yelled Egon.

'I'm here!' shouted Ray.

They launched themselves and Ecto-2 off the bridge and hurtled down through space. With a resounding thud, they landed beside Ecto-1 in their shattered craft.

The toy monster was slipping and sliding all over the place. Caught up in Ray's rope and skidding on Slimer's cunning trail of slime, it scooped up Egon's device as it fell from the bridge and plummeted towards the water.

'SPLASHHHHHHHHHH!'

A small tidal wave went up. Then there was silence.

The Ghostbusters rushed to the edge and looked over.

All was calm. They thought they had won the day.

'That fixed him,' said Peter proudly.

But the monster was not finished yet. Out of the depths came the huge, snake-like tentacle. This time it had an enormous mouth at the tip. Vicious teeth snapped up at them.

'What happened to that device of yours, Egon?' asked Ray.

'Five seconds from now,' promised the other. He began a countdown under his breath. 'Zero!'

The explosion caused another tidal wave and turned the monster into a flash of blue light. An enormous force went through the demon and destroyed it for good, sending it to the bottom of the river with a bubbling sound.

The Ghostbusters had rescued their city yet again.

With Slimer's help.

It was their turn to be acclaimed by the crowd.

Cheers went up all round. They waved in acknowledgement. Television cameras rolled and they were seen at their moment of triumph across the whole continent.

The Ghostbusters were the best once more.

Peter Venkman turned to Slimer and grinned.

'Slimer, I hate to say this,' he began, but – you looked mah-vellous!'

Slimer gave him a big, slobbery kiss of thanks.

'Yuck!' said Peter. 'I been slimed!'

Slimer giggled merrily. He was among friends again.

'Gug-gug-gug-gug!'

Winston stepped forward and winked an eye.

'Now this is what I call a happy ending!'

'Not for everybody,' said Ray.

He held up the ghost-trap and they heard voices inside.

'Did we win, Pop?' asked Zonk.

'Aw, shuddup!' snarled Slug.

Ghosts-R-Us was history.

If you have enjoyed GHOSTS-R-US, you might like to read the other *Real Ghostbuster* titles from Knight Books:

A Royal Mail service in association with the Book Marketing Council & The Booksellers Association.

Post-A-Book is a Post Office trademark.

THE REAL GHOSTBUSTERS No. 1

JANINE'S GENIE

by Kenneth Harper

When a client offers the Ghostbusters the pick
of his belongings instead of payment, Janine
chooses a ridiculous, old brass oil-lamp and
unleashes a load of trouble on to town, in the
shape of a lampful of ghosts and ghouls.

KNIGHT BOOKS

Coming soon – to save the world –

THE REAL GHOSTBUSTERS No. 3

SLIMER, COME HOME

by Kenneth Harper

When Slimer eats one cake too many, such
is his shame that he leaves his Ghostbuster
companions and turns, in his loneliness, to
some new – and dangerous – friends . . .

KNIGHT BOOKS

GH⊙STBUSTERS™

novelisation by Larry Milne

(based on the screenplay by
Dan Aykroyd and Harold Ramis)

Who or what can deliver New York from the dreaded tyranny of the paranormal? Who can save the city from a plague of ghosts that will spare no living creature and leave no street unvisited?

Who but a half crazed trio called the Ghostbusters. Poised between genius and lunacy, these cosmic crusaders alone have the power to combat a force unknown to human kind . . .

CORONET

novelisation by Kenneth Harper

Welcome to the World of MASK – Mobile Armoured Strike Kommand where illusion and deception team up with man and machine.

There are eight stunning Mask adventures from KNIGHT Books.

☑	39890 6	MASK 1 – The Deathstone	£1.95
☑	39891 4	MASK 2 – Peril Under Paris	£1.95
☑	39892 2	MASK 3 – Venice Menace	£1.95
☐	39977 5	MASK 4 – Book of Power	£1.95
☑	40327 6	MASK 5 – Panda Power	£1.95
☐	41535 5	MASK 6 – The Plunder of Glow-worm Grotto	£1.95
☐	41534 7	MASK 7 – The Everglades Oddity	£1.95
☐	41684 X	MASK 8 – Dragonfire	£1.95

All these books are available at your local bookshop or newsagent, or can be ordered direct from the publisher. Just tick the titles you want and fill in the form at the end.

Prices and availability subject to change without notice.

Hodder and Stoughton Paperbacks, P.O. Box 11, Falmouth, Cornwall.

Please send cheque or postal order, and allow the following for postage and packing:

U.K. – 55p for one book, plus 22p for the second book, and 14p for each additional book ordered up to a £1.75 maximum.

B.F.P.O. and EIRE – 55p for the first book, plus 22p for the second book, and 14p per copy for the next 7 books, 8p per book thereafter.

OTHER OVERSEAS CUSTOMERS – £1.00 for the first book, plus 25p per copy for each additional book.

Name ....

Address ....

....